Introduction

Easy to Make! Easy to Read!

Young children get excited reading about things that relate to their everyday experiences. But they get even more excited when they can help create the art and text in these reading materials. The books in the *Make Your Own Emergent Readers* series provide children with interactive, personalized reading experiences by inviting them to investigate, complete sentence frames, illustrate, put together, and create covers for their very own readers. Each book in the series contains 10 eight-page themed reproducible books for emergent readers. These easy-to-read Little Books contain text that is simple, predictable, and repetitive, and usually have one or two new words or changes on each page. The books present various subject matter following a specific theme.

This resource, *At the Zoo*, provides everything you need to get children excited about reading as they create their very own library of self-made and illustrated zoo books.

This book includes:

Creative Suggestions and Activities

Pages 3–7 provide creative suggestions and activities for each Little Book, including:

Cover Idea—Tells you how to create a colorful, eye-catching cover using a variety of art techniques and mediums.

Ideas for Illustrating Inside Pages—Help you guide children to add their own text to many of the books and creatively illustrate the pages.

Extension Activities—Provide unique ways to extend learning concepts presented in the Little Books as well as encourage further reading and writing.

Literature List

A comprehensive list of related books is provided on page 8. Use these books as read-alouds, research material, and extra books children can read on their own. Theme-related read-alouds enhance your literacy program by providing background knowledge and extending the concepts introduced in the content areas.

Directions for Making the Little Books

Putting the Pages Together

Reproduce the pages for each Little Book. *Do not cut pages in half!* Children can fold the pages and place them in numerical order. The pages will be doubled, and text will read on both sides. This unique page construction creates more durable books for frequent rereading. Also, creating artwork is easier. Markers and paint will not bleed through, and the pages are more suitable for collage materials.

Note: Depending on the art technique used, it may be easier for children to illustrate each page before assembling books, especially if it's a messy technique! Have extra pages available for "mess-ups." Once the art is complete and pages are in order, fold the pages on the dotted line and bind them together. Stapling is the easiest, but pages can also be hole-punched and bound with ribbon or yarn.

Adding a Cover and Completing the Pages

- The first page of each Little Book can serve as the cover. However, you may choose to follow the cover suggestions on pages 3–7, or invite children to each make a special, individualized cover of his or her own. Make two covers at a time by cutting 12" x 18" (30 cm x 45 cm) construction paper in half lengthwise, and then folding each piece in half.

- The inside pages can be illustrated quickly and easily by drawing and/or coloring. (Refer to the Literature List on page 8 for books that help children learn to draw.) Peruse pages 3–7 for directions (in many instances, children are asked to complete existing art and/or draw inside borders or frames) and suggestions for implementing creative, visually-exciting art techniques. These suggestions are a great way to integrate the arts into your program, and children will love experimenting with collage materials, pastels, paint, crayon-resist, cut paper, and more!

- In advance, make several photocopies of your class picture. Children can use their own pictures whenever a self-portrait or photo is called for in the art. Or, you can use photocopied pictures to create a "Meet the Author" page for special books.

- You may also attach a "comments" page on the inside back covers of the books. Here children can dictate or write their feelings about the book, what they learned, or more text additions to continue the story.

- To encourage rereading, attach a page to the inside back covers on which children can list the people to whom they have read their books.

Using the Little Books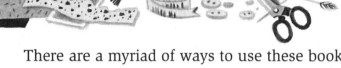

Before children make and read Little Books on their own, introduce them to the text during shared reading activities. Depending on children's reading-skill development, they should have several opportunities to interact with the text before making each Little Book. You can do this in a variety of ways:

- Make a class big book using the text from the Little Book combined with student illustrations. Read the big book several times during shared reading time.

- Make a pocket chart of the Little Book's text, along with matching picture cards.

- Make overhead transparencies of the Little Book's text and art.

Just think of how proud children will be showing off their own creatively-designed books to their classmates and families!

There are a myriad of ways to use these books in your classroom and at home, but here are just a few suggestions on how to incorporate the Little Books into your literacy program:

- Learning-center activities
- Extra reading in the content areas
- As an introduction to various subjects
- Independent reading material
- Homework activities
- Reading material for the child at home
- Practice with sight words

Creative Suggestions and Activities

Where Am I?

Cover Idea

On the cover, write or cut out the title in large, colorful letters. Give clues to the content of the book by drawing and coloring your favorite zoo animals peeking out from around the letters.

Inside Pages

Refer to zoo and animal books to find out each animal's correct coloring, and then color the animals as realistically as possible. On page 8, draw your favorite zoo animal(s).

Extension Activities

- After learning about zoo animals, brainstorm with children additional lines of text for each page. Write the text on paper strips and attach them to the book pages to extend reading.

- Create a class zoo. Invite children to bring in animal models and realistic stuffed animals. Separate the animals according to common habitats and create simple backdrops. Label the animals and write interesting facts about them on index cards. Invite other classes to visit your class zoo!

- Write a "How?" book explaining how each animal got its unique characteristics. (Read Rudyard Kipling's *The Elephant Child*.) For example, a child can tell how a zebra got its stripes or how a giraffe got its long neck.

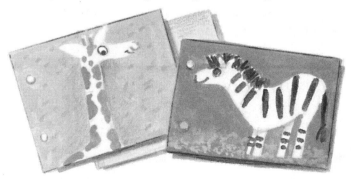

We're Off to the Zoo!

Cover Idea

Create the cover by cutting a school bus from yellow construction paper. Add pictures of yourself and your classmates in the windows of the bus. If you are taking a trip to the zoo through books and films, design a magic school bus that will transport you there and back.

Inside Pages

On page 3, write in the speech bubbles which animals you would most like to see at the zoo; for example, *I want to see a boa constrictor!* or *I want to see a penguin!* For the rest of the book, insert blank pages in between the Little Book pages so you can add your own drawings matching the text descriptions (e.g., big animals, small animals, tall animals, short animals). Finally, on page 8, draw what you would most like to see or do at the zoo.

Extension Activities

- Before going on a trip to the zoo, create a chart with three columns. In the first column, list what children already know about the zoo. In the second column, list what children want to learn about the zoo. After your trip to the zoo, list the new things children learned in the third column.

- With children, make a list of predictions about what you will see and do at the zoo. After your trip, read your predictions, check the ones that actually transpired, and make another list of other things you saw and did. Have children make an innovation of the Little Book titled *We're Back from the Zoo!*, and write about and illustrate what they saw and did at the zoo.

Elephants

Cover Idea

Create an elephant for the cover by cutting simple shapes from gray construction paper or Fun Foam and gluing them together. Add a wiggly eye to the elephant's head. Use construction-paper scraps to create details.

Inside Pages

Make the elephants as fun and colorful as you wish! They can be purple or pink, polka-dotted or striped! Outline the elephants on each page with black crayon and then watercolor within the black lines. On page 8, draw your own fanciful elephant. Maybe you can even be taking a ride on its back!

Extension Activities

- Draw a large elephant on butcher paper and outline it with black marker. Paint the elephant using tan or gray tempera paint. When the paint dries, cut out the elephant. Using black marker, write on facts and information you learned about elephants during your theme study. Display your elephant on a bulletin board.

- Research with children the similarities and differences between Asian and African elephants. Record your findings on the board in a Venn diagram.

- Challenge children with "elephant math"! Invite them to find out the length of an elephant's ears, nose, body, and so on. Use Unifix cubes to measure each length. Then have children measure their own corresponding body parts and compare lengths. Invite them to make a book of comparisons, including text such as *An elephant's nose is _____ Unifix cubes long, but mine is only three.*

Bears Are Everywhere!

Cover Idea

Use a dark blue cover and colored paper scraps to design an environment for your favorite bear. Then lightly sketch your bear and sponge-paint it with tempera. When the paint is dry, add details with black marker.

Inside Pages

Research more about bears. Use the information to color the bears as realistically as possible. You can even add fuzzy fabric to make each bear "fluffy." On page 8, draw your favorite zoo bear.

Extension Activities

- Locate where different bears live on a world map or globe. After reading more about the bears in the story, discuss how they have adapted to the areas where they live.

- Create a class book of bears. Find out several more facts about the bears in the story and other bears as well. Use tempera to paint the bears in their natural habitats and add several lines of informational text to each page.

- Have children search the library for fictional books about bears. Make your classroom the "den of good bear books." Challenge children to read as many books as they can. Give each child a bear cutout every time he or she reads one. Have children write their names and the book titles on the cutouts, and create a bear chain around the classroom!

Monkey See, Monkey Do

Cover Idea

Tear strips of brown construction paper or lunch sacks for tree trunks, and glue them to a blue cover. Tear and glue on green construction-paper "leaves" and "grass." Add playful monkeys to the scene using peanut shells as the monkeys' bodies. Draw details with black marker, and add brown yarn tails.

Extension Activities

- Gather books and magazines about monkeys. Have children use the materials to write and illustrate a class nonfiction book about the monkeys featured in the Little Book.

- Children love to play "Monkey See, Monkey Do." Invite one child "leader" to make hand or body movements for the rest of the class to mimic. This is great for when you have a few minutes to fill between activities.

- Create "life-sized" monkeys! For each monkey, cut five 3" x 18" (7.5 cm x 45 cm) brown construction-paper strips and round the corners. These will be the legs, arms, and tail. Have children trace their hands and bare feet onto brown paper and glue them to the "arms" and "legs." For the body, round the corners of 9" x 18" (22.5 cm x 45 cm) brown paper. Make a slightly smaller oval from tan paper and glue it to the brown oval. Make the head by rounding the corners of 9" x 9" (22.5 cm x 22.5 cm) brown paper, then add a 6" x 9"(15 cm x 22.5 cm) tan oval for the mouth. Cut and paste on eyes and ears, and fill in details with crayons. Attach the arms, legs, tail, and head to the body with brads. Hang monkeys around the room in various positions to create your own jungle!

Zoo Cats

Cover Idea

Make a lion's head from a small paper plate for the cover. Paint the plate with yellow tempera mixed with brown. Add facial features and ears cut from construction paper. Tear yellow and orange tissue paper into strips and glue them around the lion's head as a mane.

Inside Pages

When assembling the Little Book, insert blank pages. On these pages, draw and color your own pictures of big cats in their natural habitats. Do some research and write new text about each cat.

Extension Activities

- Make a colorful cat mural! Invite children to sketch different cats with chalk on a long sheet of black butcher paper. Make drawings big and bold, avoiding small detail. Trace over children's drawings with white glue. When the glue is dry, have children color inside the glue lines with oil pastels or colored chalk. To avoid smearing, spray with hair spray or fixative in a well-ventilated area. If you wish, add facts about the cats on sentence strips.

- Have children add a page to their Little Books about house cats. Have them write about what domestic cats like to do, where they sleep, and how they play.

FS-69005 At the Zoo

My Visit to the Zoo

Cover Idea

Make a cover from lightweight tagboard. Draw a background with a wild animal design or glue on wild animal wrapping paper or wallpaper samples.  Add the title and a picture of yourself taken at the zoo or at the classroom zoo. For added fun, take the photo wearing a safari hat and vest.

Inside Pages

This book makes a great keepsake of a trip to the zoo, either real or imaginary. Finish the text with ways you experienced the zoo through your five senses. Draw and color pictures to go with each page, or add photos. On page 8, write about and illustrate what you learned at the zoo.

Extension Activities

- On your field trip to the zoo, have children bring pencils and clipboards. Invite them to jot notes about what they experience through their five senses. When you return to school, make a class mural of the zoo, referring to children's notes. Make the mural interactive by adding "lift-and-look" flaps. Include animals hidden behind trees and bushes, underground, or in water. Add animal sounds in speech bubbles, then write out several sentence strips describing children's experiences. Add these sentences to your mural.

- Invite children to write a book titled *My Favorite Things at the Zoo*. Brainstorm a category for each page, such as animals, food, shows, exhibits, and so on. For example, *My favorite animal at the zoo is the tiger; My favorite food at the zoo is cotton candy;* or *My favorite exhibit at the zoo is the snake house.*

Zoo Sounds

Cover Idea

Design a colorful border around the cover using ribbon, rick-rack, glitter, and construction-paper scraps. Add the title,  then create a collage of "zoo-animal noises," such as *ROAR, GROWL, BARK,* and *HISSSS.* Use magazine cutout letters, stamps, glitter glue, and puffy paint. Trace the words with colorful markers.

Inside Pages

Refer to the drawing books (see Literature List, page 8) for help in drawing animals. Then draw the appropriate animal for each page, adding a speech bubble with the noise that animal makes, such as *GROWL!* on page 1 and *ROAR!* on page 2.

Extension Activities

- The book *Polar Bear, Polar Bear, What Do You Hear?* by Bill Martin, Jr. and Eric Carle is a wonderful book about the zoo and animal noises. Create a class version of the book using animals you learned about or saw at the zoo. For example, *Giraffe, giraffe, what do you hear? I hear a monkey chattering in my ear.* Add brightly-colored animal collages, like Carle's, as illustrations.

- Make a new book called *More Zoo Sounds!* or *Pet Sounds!* Invite children to brainstorm other animals and their noises, for example, *The seal says, "Bark!" The kitten says, "Meow!"*

What Do Zookeepers Do at the Zoo?

Cover Idea

Cut out an upper-body shape and attach it to the cover. Color or glue on a brown or green fabric uniform shirt and add a zoo badge with the worker's name. Add yarn or tissue-paper hair and facial features. Then draw the animal the zookeeper cares for.

Inside Pages

On page 2, draw the animal you would most like to care for if you were a zookeeper. And on page 8, illustrate how you could be this animal's best friend. Add an extra page at the back of the book. Research your animal and write about how you would care for it. In what habitat does your animal live? What kind of food does it eat?

Extension Activities

- When arranging a zoo field trip, set up a short interview with a zookeeper, so children can learn more about his or her job.
- Have children use the Little Book's format to write innovations about teachers, nurses, moms and dads, police officers, and so on.
- Assign a student zookeeper to each animal in the classroom zoo (see *Where Am I?*, page 3). Have "zookeepers" research how to care for their animals, and give short oral reports about what they learned.

Guess Who's at the Zoo

Cover Idea

Decorate the cover with a large question mark cut from animal-print wrapping paper or wallpaper. Draw and color zoo animals peeking from behind the question mark. Add zoo animal stickers or animal stampings to finish the design.

Inside Pages

Illustrate each page with the appropriate animal, then write and illustrate your own animal riddle on page 8. Add a "lift-and-look" flap to each page, so the reader can guess the animal before looking.

Extension Activities

- Invite each child to make a zoo animal headband. Make sure a variety of animals are represented. Help children find several facts about their animals for an oral report. Invite them to wear their headbands when presenting their reports to the class.
- Share the bold, graphic art by Eric Carle in *1, 2, 3 to the Zoo* and *Polar Bear, Polar Bear, What Do You Hear?* Invite children to experiment with his technique using finger paints, finger-paint paper, butcher paper, and paintbrushes. Have children paint with bright colors. When the paint dries, draw and cut out various zoo animals. Display children's artwork in a special exhibit in the school.
- Make paper-plate masks of animals in the Little Book. Invite children to present the book to other classes, with each "mystery animal" wearing a mask and hiding under a box painted as a zoo sign. Elicit guesses from students to make the unveiling of the "animal" dramatic. Keep score of correct guesses and give animal cookies as prizes!

Literature List

Any Bear Can Wear Glasses: The Spectacled Bear & Other Curious Creatures by Matthew and Thomas Long (Chronicle Books)

At the Zoo by Douglas Florian (Greenwillow)

Baby Animals Series by Kate Petty (Barron)

The Beauty of the Beast: Poems from the Animal Kingdom by Jack Prelutsky (Knopf)

Biggest, Strongest, Fastest by Steve Jenkins (Ticknor & Fields)

The Children's Animal Atlas by David Lambert (Millbrook Press)

Color Zoo by Lois Ehlert (Lippincott)

Curious George Visits the Zoo by Margaret Rey (Houghton Mifflin)

Furry Alphabet Book by Jerry Pallotta (Children's Press)

Giraffe by Mary Ling (Dorling Kindersley)

Giraffes by Bobbie Kalman (Crabtree)

Going to the Zoo by Tom Paxton (Morrow)

If I Ran the Zoo by Dr. Seuss (Random House)

My Visit to the Zoo by Aliki (HarperCollins)

1, 2, 3 to the Zoo by Eric Carle (Philomel)

The Opposite Zoo by Steven Walker (Puffin Books)

Peek-a-Boo at the Zoo: New Reader Series by Frank B. Edwards (Bungalo Books)

Polar Bear, Polar Bear, What Do You Hear? by Bill Martin, Jr. (Holt)

Put Me in the Zoo by Robert Lopshire (Random House)

V for Vanishing: An Alphabet of Endangered Animals by Patricia Mullins (HarperCollins)

Zoo by Gail Gibbons (HarperCollins)

The Zoo at Night: Verses by Michael Rosen (Tradewind Books)

Zoobooks Series (Wildlife Education Ltd.)

Zoo Clues: Making the Most of Your Visit to the Zoo by Sheldon L. Gerstenfeld (Puffin Books)

Zoo Day by Jon Brennan (Carolrhoda)

Zoo Doings: Animal Poems by Jack Prelutsky (Greenwillow)

The Zookeeper's Sleepers: New Reader Series by Frank B. Edwards (Bungalo Books)

Zoos by Daniel and Susan Cohen (Doubleday)

Videos

Bonkers for Babies with Jack Hanna (Time Life)

Desert Animals from the *See How They Grow Series* (Sony)

Jungle from *Eyewitness Series* (DK Vision)

Jungle Animals from the *See How They Grow Series* (Sony)

Really Wild Animals Series (National Geographic)

Talking with the Animals with Jack Hanna (Time Life)

What's Up, Down, Under? Zoo Life with Jack Hanna (Time Life)

Wild Animals from the *See How They Grow Series* (Sony)

Zoo (Smithsonian)

Drawing Books

Draw Fifty Series by Lee J. Ames (Doubleday)

Ed Emberley's Drawing Book: Make a World by Ed Emberley (Little, Brown)

Ed Emberley's Drawing Book of Animals by Ed Emberley (Little, Brown)

Ed Emberley's Great Thumbprint Drawing Book by Ed Emberley (Little, Brown)

Ed Emberley's Picture Pie: A Book of Circle Art by Ed Emberley (Little, Brown)

I Can Draw Series by Lisa Bonforte (Simon & Schuster)

FS-69005 At the Zoo

Where Am I? written by Rozanne Lanczak Williams

I see a zebra.

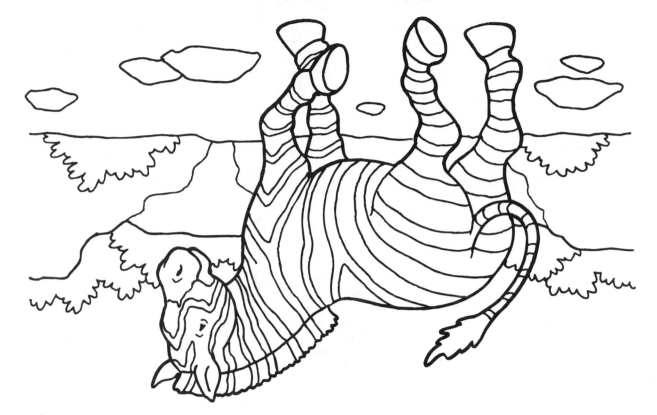

Where Am I?

spider monkey

tree frog

sloth

toucan

tree boa

1

I see a giraffe.

© Frank Schaffer Publications, Inc.

I see chimpanzees.
They make me laugh!

Where Am I? written by Rozanne Lanczak Williams

9

I see lots of animals
with fur and four paws.

lynx

panda

hyena

wolf

macaw

puffin

flamingo

I see flamingos, puffins,
and colorful macaws.

5

Where Am I? written by Rozanne Lanczak Williams

I see a koala and a kangaroo.

Where am I?

7

We're Off to the Zoo! written by Rozanne Lanczak Williams

Get ready, get set,
We're off to the zoo!

We're Off to the

ring-tailed lemur

toucan

penguin

green tree python

1

What will we do?

What will we see?

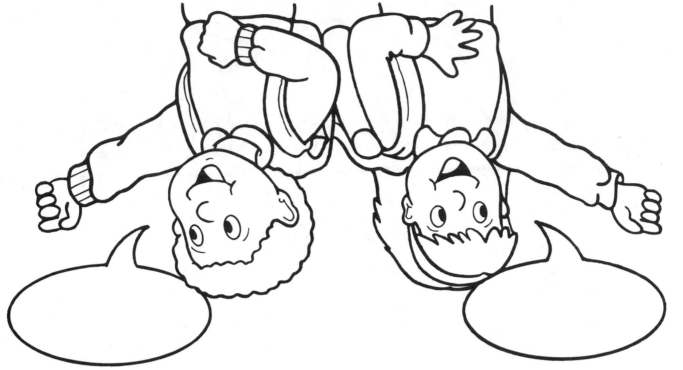

African elephant

lesser mouse lemur

pygmy
marmoset

rhinoceros

We'll see lots of animals,
Big ones and small.

4

Lions and tigers
And bears, oh, my!

lion

cinnamon bear

Siberian tiger

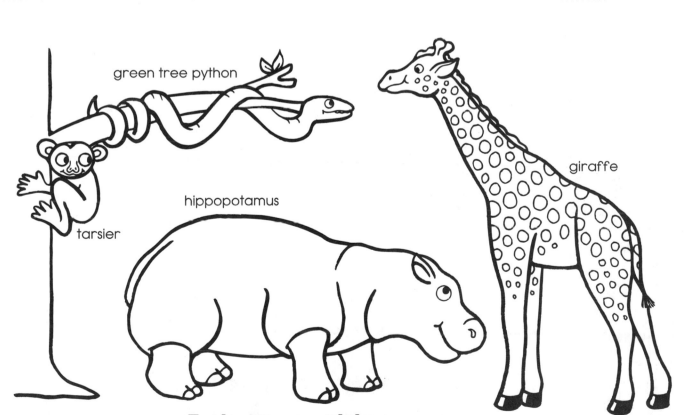

green tree python

giraffe

hippopotamus

tarsier

**Fat ones, skinny ones,
Short ones, and tall.**

Animals that swim,
And fly in the sky.

7

alligator

platypus

toucan

cockatiel

© Frank Schaffer Publications, Inc.

gazelle

Get ready, get set,
We're off to the zoo!
What will we see? What will we do?

8

We're Off to the Zoo! written by Rozanne Lanczak Williams

2

And they're terribly fat.
They're terribly big,
Elephants walk like this and that.

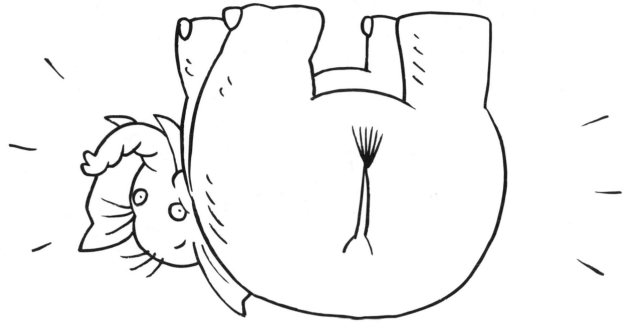

Elephants

And they're terribly fat.
They're terribly big,

1

3

They have no fingers,
And they have no toes.

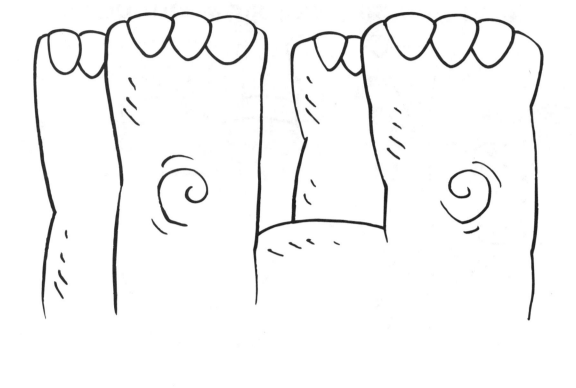

4

But oh my goodness, what a nose!

Elephants adapted by Rozanne Lanczak Williams

They play in the water,
And roll in the sand.

**Elephants are the biggest
that live on land.**

They're terribly smart,
And they're terribly strong.

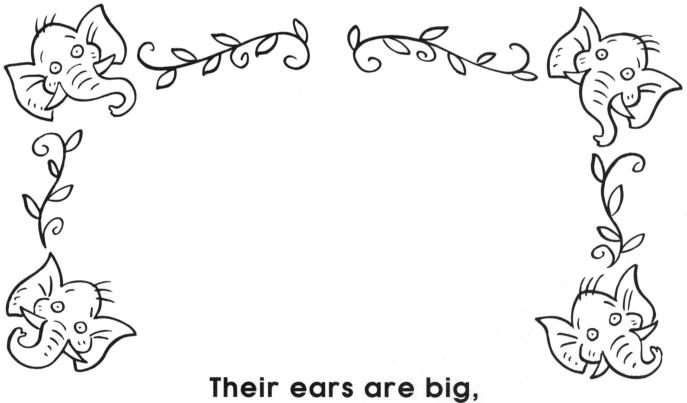

Their ears are big,
And their trunks are long!

Bears Are Everywhere! written by Rozanne Lanczak Williams

2

Bears at the zoo are everywhere!

I see a bear here. I see a bear there.

1

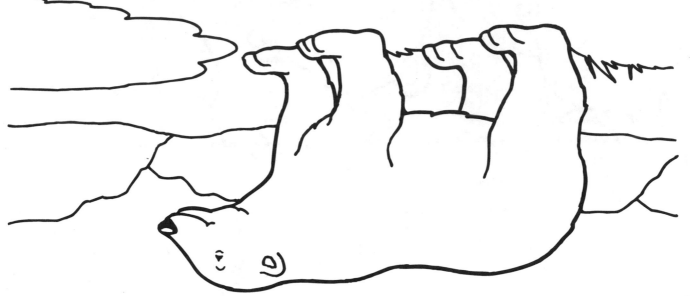

3

They are the best hunters of all bears.

Polar bears live on top of the world.

I see a polar bear.

I see a grizzly bear.

Grizzly bears are brown with long claws.

They live in North America.

4

Bears Are Everywhere! written by Rozanne Lanczak Williams

6   Their long tongues lap up termites. Yum!

Malayan sun bears are the smallest bears.

I see a Malayan sun bear.

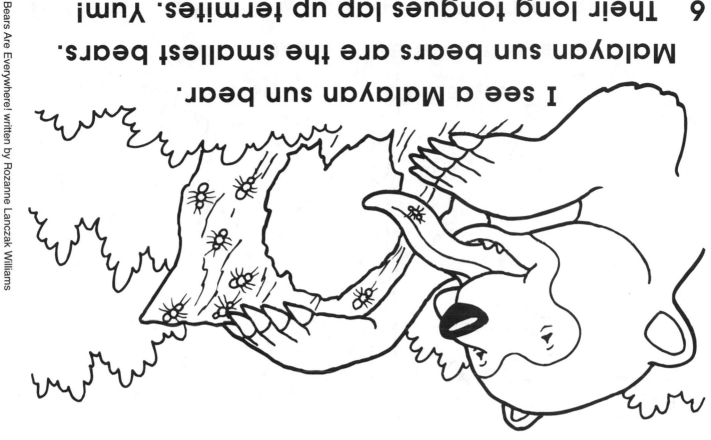

I see a spectacled bear.

Spectacled bears look like they wear glasses.

They live in South America.   5

They climb trees when they are in danger.
Black bears live in forests.
I see a black bear.

I see a bear here. I see a bear there.
Bears at the zoo are everywhere!

8

Monkey See, Monkey Do written by Rozanne Lanczak Williams

2

I like monkeys at the zoo!

Monkey see, monkey do.

lowland gorillas

Monkey See

Monkey Do

spider monkey

1

Monkeys talk.

3

© Frank Schaffer Publications, Inc.

Monkeys play.

4

I could watch them play all day!

Monkey See, Monkey Do written by Rozanne Lanczak Williams

Little baby monkeys cling.

olive baboons

orangutans

Monkeys grin.

Monkeys swing.

Watching monkeys is a treat!
Monkeys sleep. Monkeys eat.

lion-tailed macaques

squirrel monkey

red howler monkey

golden
lion tamarin

colobus monkey

proboscis monkey

Monkey see, monkey do.

I like monkeys at the zoo!

Zoo Cats written by Rozanne Lanczak Williams

Cheetahs are the fastest runners.

This cat is a cheetah.

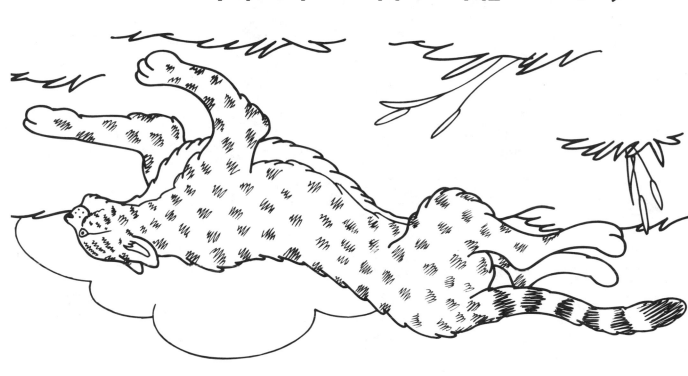

Spanish lynx

ZOO CATS

3

Snow leopards are the rarest cats.

This cat is a snow leopard.

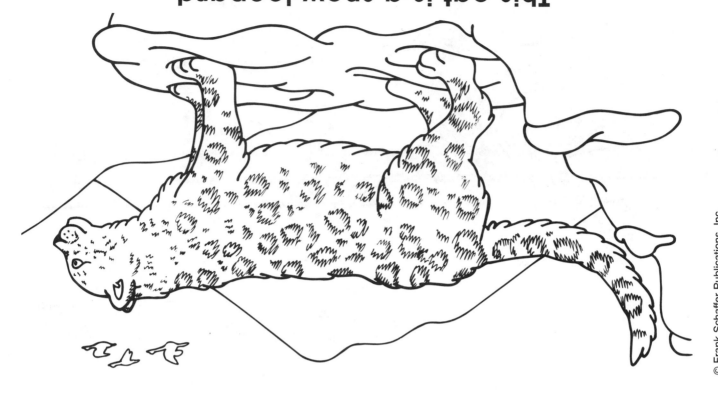

These cats are lions.

4 Lions are the only cats that live in groups.

Zoo Cats written by Rozanne Lanczak Williams

5

These groups are called prides.

6 Tigers like to splash and play in water.

They are the biggest cats.

These cats are Siberian tigers.

© Frank Schaffer Publications, Inc.

Zoo Cats written by Rozanne Lanczak Williams

This cat is a leopard.
Leopards store their food in trees
until they are hungry.

This cat is a jaguar.
Jaguars' spots hide
them when they hunt.

Zoo Cats written by Rozanne Lanczak Williams

2 I visited the zoo on _____.

SUNDAY MONDAY
TUESDAY WEDNESDAY THURSDAY
FRIDAY SATURDAY

My Visit to the Zoo

By _____

1

There were lots of sights to see.

3   I saw _____.

There were lots of sounds to hear.

4   I heard _____.

© Frank Schaffer Publications, Inc.

My Visit to the Zoo written by Rozanne Lanczak Williams

6

I touched _____.

There were lots of things to touch.

There were lots of smells to smell.

I smelled_____.

5

There were lots of foods to taste.

I tasted _____ .

7

© Frank Schaffer Publications, Inc.

There were lots of things to learn.

8   I learned _____ .

My Visit to the Zoo written by Rozanne Lanczak Williams

Lions roar.

Zoo Sounds written by Rozanne Lanczak Williams

© Frank Schaffer Publications, Inc.

Zoo Sounds

Bears growl.

1

Parrots squawk in the trees.

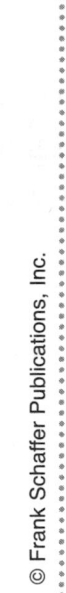

Hyenas roll around
and laugh tee, hee, hee!

Monkeys screech.

Rhinos snort.

Snakes hiss and slither on the ground.

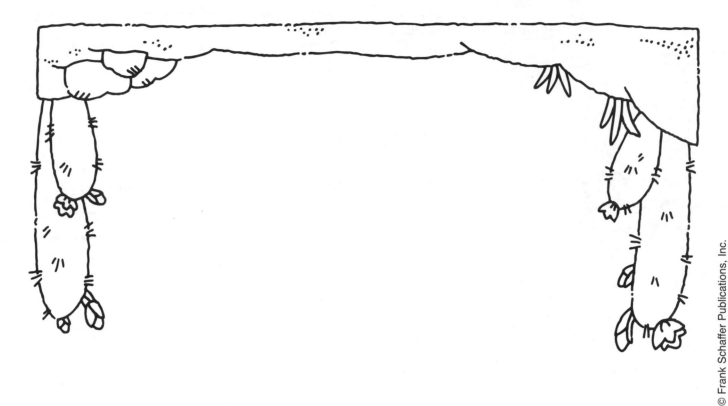

8   **Sounds at the zoo are all around!**

What Do Zookeepers Do at the Zoo?

Each zookeeper takes care of

one kind of animal.

Zookeepers prepare special food for the animals.

© Frank Schaffer Publications, Inc.

Zookeepers clean and groom the animals.

8   I am a _____.

I _____.

I _____.

I live in Asia and Africa.

I have very thick skin and a horn on my nose.

I am a _____.

7

5

I am a(n) _____.

I look just like I did 200 million years ago.

I am one of the largest reptiles in the world.

I am the biggest bird but I can't fly.

I lay eggs in an 8-foot nest in the ground.

6   I am an _____.

4

I have a very long neck.

I live on the plains of Africa.

I am a _____.

I look like a bear, but I am a marsupial.

I live in Australia and eat eucalyptus leaves.

I am a _____.

3

1

Guess Who's at the Zoo

I am the biggest animal that lives on land.

I use my nose to smell, grab, and drink.

2   I am an _____.

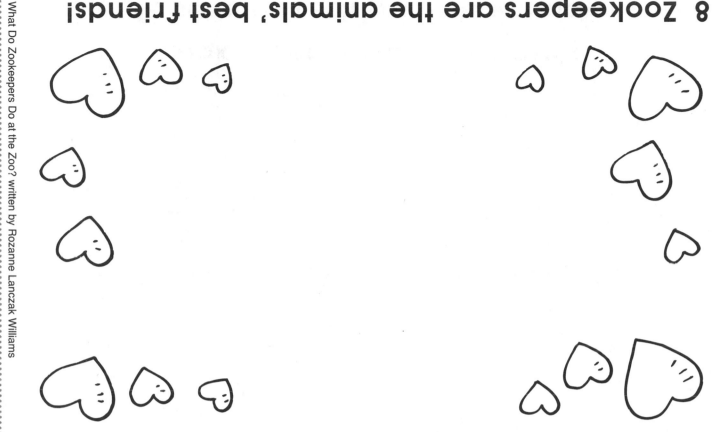

Zookeepers carefully watch and care for
the animals' babies when they are born.   7

Zookeepers give the animals
food and fresh water each day.

**Zookeepers work with veterinarians
to take care of sick animals.**

What Do Zookeepers Do at the Zoo? written by Rozanne Lanczak Williams